Jenny Oldfield

my little life

When Geri and I fell out

illustrated by Martina Farrow

Hodder
Children's
Books

a division of Hodder Headline Limited

Text copyright © 2002 Jenny Oldfield
Illustrations copyright © 2002 Martina Farrow
Cover illustration © 2002 Nila Aye

First published in Great Britain in 2002
by Hodder Children's Books

A Catalogue record for this book is available from the British Library

ISBN 0 340 85074 4

Printed and bound in Great Britain by
Bookmarque Ltd, Croydon, Surrey

Hodder Children's Books
A division of Hodder Headline Limited
338 Euston Road, London NW1 3BH

A big thank you to the hundreds of kids I met
on school visits who helped me with ideas
for these books!

Thursday, December 15th

No I'm not, and I haven't. Why do they make lurve sound like chicken-pox?

According to Destiny Diva, it's a match made in snog heaven. Have practised making kissy lips in the mirror, just in case.

Have also completed puzzle page, entered a competition to win a DVD player and read the horoscopes twice. Still can't get to sleep.

11.00p.m. Have started a new short story:

'As she watched the funeral carriage enter the iron gates of the graveyard, Marie-Nicole knew that life would never be the same again.'

Story will be in flashbacks about Marie-Nicole's mother's tragic and star-crossed love affair with a

French count. The date is 1789. People are having their heads lopped off by the guillotine. Marie-Nicole's widowed mum is a candle-maker's daughter. Falling in love with Count Montmartre is a betrayal of her working-class roots at a time of bloody rebellion . . .

Chop, chop, chop – the heads of the lords and ladies roll, so Angelique (Marie-Nicole's mum) hides her lover in the cellar of her father's house . . .

I've got it all worked out in my head.

12.30a.m. Still no sleep. Have even counted sheep.

The truth is, I've got a mega embarrassing problem. Not the kind you talk about, even to your best friend. May have to write whinging, pathetic letter to advice page.

'Dear Gabrielle,
Am I a freak? I used to be bra size 30A, but I've shrunk a whole half a cup size! Does this happen to other girls? Will my friends laugh at me in the changing rooms?'

8

'Dear Tiffany,

I'm sorry to hear about your embarra-tastic ailment. As you know, most babes of your age gradually go up in size in that department. Are you sure you've measured right? If so, and the truth is that they really are vanishing, I suggest a visit to the doctor to help you come to terms with this freakish and probably irreversible complaint. Meanwhile, try stuffing your 30A bra with loo paper. Good luck, Gabrielle.'

Have tried the loo paper trick, and hope it'll work. No gym lesson until Monday, thank the Lord!

1.00 a.m. Go to sleep! Brain, stop thinking! I wish you could click a switch inside your head. Click – Zzzzz!

Ten minutes ago, I heard Dad go downstairs to make himself a cuppa. Crept down after him and asked for hot chocolate.

'What's up, Tiff? Can't you sleep either?' he asked. His hair was sticking up at the back, he was in his T-shirt and boxers.

We sat at the table, listening to the kettle boil.

9

Compared with Dad, my problems are tiny (ha ha!).

Am back in bed. Will count kangaroos instead.

Friday, December 16th

Your stars – *Give yourself a makeover for the weekend – funky fun hair, candy-floss pink lippy and a slinky, silver, strappy top. Cool!*

Ugh! Brain feels like Play-dough, eyes look like slices of green gherkin. DID NOT GET ENOUGH SLEEP! Am not thinking of going anywhere in slinky, strappy anything, not with my unfortunate ailment!

Bad breath Bud came upstairs and pounced on me at six a.m. (Dad left kitchen door open and the crafty canine snuck up early).

Scott hogged the bathroom for thirty-five minutes, and this is my brother I'm talking about – the kid who has lived for fifteen years with a serious water allergy. Now, suddenly he takes twenty-minute showers and uses all my Grapefruit and Mango Body Shop shampoo. 'Luurve-lurv-lu-u-urve!' Dad sings a Beatles song outside the door. Scott slams things and comes out in a cloud of steam.

(N.B. Yesterday I saw him looking in the Yellow Pages for Tattooists. 'Don't do it, Scott!' I cried. 'Think how horrible it'll look when you're old and wrinkly!'

I have to be the voice of common sense around here. (Or, as dear Scott sees it, 'a right old bag!') It was only when I told him how painful getting a tattoo was that he closed the phone book and switched on the telly instead. Scott says he has a 'low pain threshold'. Meaning, he's a lily-livered, yellow-bellied, cringing coward. Aaargh, mi hearties!)

11

I went into the bathroom fully clothed, brushed teeth, then wiped the full-length mirror clear of steam. I wanted to look at myself sideways on, and have decided that yes, definitely, will go for cosmetic enhancement when I'm older, (say thirteen and a half) if things don't improve.

Weird, have not been worried by what I see in mirrors until recently. Have become a body-fashion victim, if there is such a thing. And it's down to the mags, I know it is! Will throw out all copies stacked up inside my wardrobe when I get back from school.

Mum rang to remind me it was her weekend. I asked her if I could bring Geri. She said she'd think about it and let me know later.

Friday evening

'Dear Gabrielle,

Can you help me? I have three best mates called Ellie (total babe), Geri (girl power) and Fuchsia (arty type). I've invited Geri to stay at Mum's place with me for the weekend. Now Ellie and Fuchsia are in a huff. What can I do to get the whole gang back together?'

'Dear Tiff,
Lucky old you, having three best mates! Some of us don't even have one. So stop moaning, get off your butt and party, party, party!
PS. By the way, are you the same Tiffany who wrote to me about her miraculous disappearing breasts?'

Am waiting for Geri to arrive after what turned out to be a nightmare day at school.

First, some girl called Nadia comes up to me and asks me to give a note to Scott. I say I don't know anyone called Scott, and she says she means my brother, and I go, 'Wot!!! That Scott!' Squealer and Chucky are earwigging and nearly wet themselves. 'Wot . . . that Scott! Wot . . . that Scott! Doh!'

Nadia (small, hard-faced, with black, sticky-out hair) goes red and punches me in the stomach as she pushes the note into my hand. What did I do to deserve that? I throw the note down the loo. Plan to tell Scott that he had a lucky escape.

Second, Nic Heron blanked me in the corridor. (OK, so I do have a crush, but this Leo chick doesn't have the guts to do anything about it. Sigh.)

Third and worst of all, I went ahead and invited Geri for the weekend. I did it during morning break, when I thought no one was around.

'I have to go to Mum's flat,' I tell her.

'What d'you mean, "have to"?' Geri's signing up for extra hockey practice at the time.

'Mum's getting a thing about access. She wants to get at Dad for some reason. Like, she was the one who left him, but she seems to have overlooked that small detail! So anyway, she wants me to stay with her more.'

'How about you? D'you wanna go?' I can see Geri's mind is on whacking a small, hard ball into a net, so I just shrug. 'It'd be cool if you could come.'

'Yeah, OK, cool. Uh-oh, where does she live?'

'Manor Road, by the bus stop. Number 16, Flat 3.'

'That's OK then. So long as I can catch a bus into school for the hockey match tomorrow morning.'

I feel as if I'm talking to an alien. I mean, who on earth would volunteer to run up and down a patch of scabby, frozen grass, being yelled at by Miss Hornby, wearing shorts and waving a wooden stick on a SATURDAY???!!!

Weird, or what?

'So, come to my place at six tonight,' I tell her.

'Do what at six?' Ellie bursts in from behind with a swish of blonde hair and a sneaky grin. She knows she's been left out of something.

The blonde hair and funky babe look is a stereotype, I realize.

But some people are. And Ellie is one. It gets people being bitchy about her, which she says is their problem, not hers. Shah, Geri and me know there's lots behind the glam surface gloss. We think . . .

'Nothing,' I mutter, not feeling like explaining when she butts in like that.

'I'm sleeping over at Tiff's mum's.' Geri comes right out with it.

Ellie goes cold and sniffy. 'Whooo, how long have you two been fixing sleepovers behind our backs? Hey, Shah, did you hear this? Maybe we should cosy up and not tell Geri and Tiff our plans for the weekend, huh?'

Ellie is not subtle. She's out there. Right out.

Shah looks embarrassed. 'I have to hand in this homework to Georgeous,' she says, and scoots off.

OK, so I messed up. Tact isn't my strong point. And Ellie took it out on me for the rest of the day, with a BIG cold shoulder for Geri and me – 'Hey, Shah, look at this! . . . Shah, did I tell you . . . ? . . . Oh, Tiff, I didn't see you standing there. Sorry I swung my bag in your face!'

The thing is, I haven't even got a 'yes' from Mum yet. She could say no, that her flat's too small, and all this will have been for nothing!

Only one good thing. We had Georgeous for English this afternoon.

Georgeous, alias Gorgeous George, aka Mr Fox.

We read *Poems from the Caribbean,* then watched a video of performance poets. They kind of sing and chant, kind of rap without music. Mega-cool.

Jenny Oldfield

Then George announced a short story writing competition. He wants us to enter in our spare time. Geri said he must be mad, expecting us to slave over our PCs when we could be rock-climbing or skateboarding. Which shows the Grand Canyon between me and Geri, cos I immediately want to enter.

Or watching a vid, Dom added. Or texting a friend, playing the latest Gameboy, shopping, listening to music, just chilling out . . .

Give George another thing (besides being cute and creative). He's sensitive too. He doesn't just concentrate on me when he's telling us about the competition. He acts as if other people will be interested too. Like maybe Callum and Shah.

The prize winner will go to London to receive a cheque from a famous writer.

Squealer: How much, sir?

Mr Fox: Fifty pounds.

Squealer: Fifty lousy quid!

Mr Fox: It's not for the cash, Adam. It's for the fame and the glory!

Squealer: Sir, I can earn fifty a day working on my dad's market stall!

Mr Fox: (*with a fake-stern stare*) Ah yes; child labour in the Undeveloped World east of Ashbrook High Street. That topic comes up in the PSE curriculum early next term, I believe!

Maths lesson, period 6. Will think about turning Marie-Nicole into my entry for the competition.

18

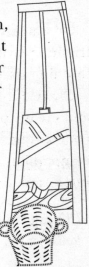

Marie-Nicole knows her mum, Angelique, is hiding Count Montmartre in the cellars under her father's candle shop. Her revolutionary grandpa wants all members of the aristocracy to be trundled off to Madame Guillotine. 'Vive la Révolution!' Angelique is desperate to save the noble count. Poor old Marie-Nicole is torn between the two:

'Her heart bled to think of her mother's sorrow if the count should be taken from her arms. And she trembled to hear the rumble of the wooden wheels of the carts which carried the dukes and duchesses to their deaths. Yet she wept for the poor of Paris. For the wretches forced to live like rats in the sewers because they had no homes. For the downtrodden servants who stole bread from their masters to feed their families.

Marie-Nicole had lived among these people for all her thirteen years. How then could she betray them now? Yet how could she bear to reveal the count's hiding place and thus break her mother's heart?'

I read Dickens's *A Tale of Two Cities* (abridged) in the half-term holiday. Sydney Carton and 'It is a far, far better thing I do now than I have ever done.' Cried loads.

Friday evening.

Geri's stars – *This week's full moon means you should take a fresh look at friendships . . .*

Ellie's stars – *Loads of planetary action means fun and frolics for you this weekend . . .*

Shah's stars – *one of your friends has been a tad depressed lately. Why not do something to put a huge smile on her face?*

Dad bought spray remedy for Bud's bad breath. Odor-eeze. Refresh Your Dog's breath in an Instant!

'It says "Insert nozzle into side of dog's mouth and press twice",' he announced, handing the white plastic bottle to me. The label has a picture of a smiling dog breathing out a cloud of flowers, like this:

I inserted and pressed once.

Bud choked. He shot out of his basket, threw his head back and howled like a wolf. Then he charged round the kitchen knocking over chairs and eventually hiding under the table, where he was sick.

'Quick, fetch a cloth!' I yelled.

Dad ran for the mop bucket under the stairs. By the time he'd filled it with water, Bud had splooshed through the sick and staggered upstairs.

'Ugh, yuck, gross!' Scott moaned from his bedroom, without lifting a finger.

Dad followed Bud with the mop. He rubbed the dog-sick into the carpet then whooshed Bud back downstairs. 'Lie down!' he barked (Dad, not Bud).

Our dog doesn't win medals for obedience. He jumped up at the kitchen table, grabbed the Odor-eeze between his jaws and scarpered into the yard.

'Tiff, phone!' Scott had raised himself from his bed, lumbered downstairs and picked up the receiver.

'Who is it?' I was outside, trying to stop Bud from burying the Odor-eeze. 'Drop it! Bad dog! Sit!'

Scrabble-scrabble, dig-dig.

'It's Mum!'

'Stay! Bad dog!' I ran back inside, where Dad was rooting in the cupboard under the sink for air freshener. Meadow Breeze. Bring a breath of the countryside into your home!

'Hi, Mum!'

'Tiff, about Geri sleeping over . . .'

'Yeah, it's OK isn't it? Cos I already organised it. She's coming round here at six.'

'I was going to say that it'll be a bit awkward. Neil will be around, and there's only one spare room, as you know.'

'Geri and me will sleep on the sofa in the living-room, no problem.' I was making faces at Scott, who was holding his nose and skidding over the greasy floor in his socks. Dad was on his hands and knees, chucking Nubuck sprays, leather-protectors, tins of polish and dusters everywhere.

'That's not the point. What's going on there? Who's making all that racket?'

'Dad. Bud's been sick. If Geri's not included, then I'm not coming either.' This was risky. These days I never know if Mum is gonna blow her top or cave in. She's going through a mid-life

crisis and blowing hot and cold over her boyfriend, Neil. Shouting or crying – you can't predict.

She sighed. 'Oh all right, have it your way. I'll pick you both up at six-fifteen.' *Slam-click-brrrr.*

Packed my bag — red top
gold top
denim skirt
grey combats
camouflage belt
clip-on red hair streaks
hairbrush
make-up
CDs
mobile phone

Bud is still in the yard, digging.

Dad never found the Meadow Breeze. I told him in the end that I'd seen Scott spraying the whole can into his smelly trainers. This led to another typical family row:

'I didn't!'

'You did!'

'Didn't!'

'Did!'

'Leave it out, you two.'

'Didn't.'

'. . . Did.'

Then Geri showed up with her new rucksack crammed with sleepover goodies, plus her hockey stick for tomorrow. She wrinkled her nose. 'What's that smell?'

'Scott's feet!' I sniggered.

'Dog sick!' he yelled.

'I said cut it out!' Dad insisted.

Then Mum arrived. She came in and stared at the chaos. Her nose twitched and her top lip curled.

'Before you ask, Bud's been sick,' Dad explained in a harassed tone.

Mum tutted, then glanced outside at the dumb, scrabbling dog. She didn't have to say that she was glad to have left this mad chaos to start a new life – you could read it in her eyes. 'Hi, Tiff! Hi, Geri!' she breezed, rising above it all. 'Let's go, huh?'

I grabbed my bag. 'Bye, Dad!'

I left him to it. Dog digging for Down-Under, brother belly-aching, kitchen turned upside down. Poor Dad.

Saturday, December 17th

Your stars – Design your own Christmas cards for friends and family. Do it now, then you'll have time to party. It's a great day for spending, flirting and snogging.

Arrived at Mum's place at 6.45. Neil was already here.

Mum put Geri and me in the spare room.

Geri taught me some karate moves from her self-defence class. Chop-chop-haa! She can get her leg up behind her ear, holding on to her ankle all the way up. She's mega double-jointed. I can press my thumb back against my wrist. Sad or what!

Then we found a hairstyle in a mag and I did her hair. Hers is long and light brown, so you can do a parting and divide it into two sections.

'"Scoop it into two high bunches",' Geri read out. She had the mag on her knee so I could see the pics. '"Check they are evenly placed on either side of your head".'

'Is that even?' I stood back and looked.

'"Take a small section of hair from one bunch and plait from top to bottom. Tie little plait with snag-free band".'

'Hold it!' I was plaiting like crazy. 'Yeah, carry on.'

'"Twist the remaining hair. Now hold the plait up and wrap the twist around the plait. Tuck away the end of the twist and pin".'

'Hang on!' I was twisting and tucking, but

Geri's hair was slippin' and slidin'. 'Where's the pin? What happens with this sticky-out bit? Whoa, was that meant to happen?'

The girl in the pics was smiling at us with her cool plaits and partings, twists and knots, funky fun hairstyle. Geri was staring in the mirror at a lopsided, straggly mess.

'Oops!' I giggled.

She grabbed the hairbrush and whacked my bum, whipping out the 'snag-free bands' and sitting me down on the chair.

'Your turn!' she cried.

So there was me, ten minutes later, gelled up to the eyeballs, glittered and sprayed, looking like a surprised hamster.

'Wacky!' Geri insisted wickedly.

Mum popped her head around the door.

'What d'you think, Mrs Little?' Geri revealed my hairstyle with a dramatic 'da-dah!'

'Great, yeah.' Mum obviously wasn't concentrating.

'So now you want me to go around looking like I've been electrocuted!' I wailed, mussing it all up.

'Tiffany, I've just had your dad on the phone.'

'What did he want?' My hair was in my eyes, I was practising karate as I followed her into the living-room (designed by Conran, super-cool).

'No, I rang him,' she said, flopping down by Neil on the (pale blue) sofa. 'I thought it was time we had a chat.'

I stopped messing. 'A chat' was serious. Neil had his head stuck in the TV Times, ignoring us. Geri was in the doorway to our room. 'And?' I asked.

'I told him I'd like you to come and stay with me for more of the time. Now that I've got the flat decorated and properly furnished and things have – well – settled down.'

Like it's a game you play whenever you feel like it! Like I'm an extra bit of the designer decor!

'That's if you want to,' Mum added. 'I said that with Scott it's different. He's older. It's not so important.'

'What did Dad say?' I whispered. I saw a lifetime of weekends with Mum and Neil stretching out in front of my eyes. Don't-spill-on-the-sofa. Don't-upset-the-posh-neighbours. Do-not-disturb!!!

'You know what he's like. He didn't say much. But at least I've broached the subject with you, haven't I, darling?' Mum settled down next to Neil, curling her legs under her, with one arm around his shoulder. 'So, that's great, isn't it?'

I didn't say anything, just went back into my room and started rehearsing dance moves with Geri. Disco divas, pop your left knee out. Tilt your head right, hands beside your face. Push your right hip out.

But Geri knew my heart wasn't in it, and we soon turned off the music and went to bed.

'At least Neil's cool,' Geri murmured across the dark room. It was the first time she'd met him and she was trying to cheer me up.

'Is he?'

'Well, OK, not "cool" exactly. But he could be worse.'

'He could?' Smarmy Mr Suit. Smooth-talking, silver-tongued . . .

Geri realized she was digging herself a hole. 'Yeah. I mean, he likes sport, doesn't he?' (Neil had demonstrated his golf swing after our Chinese takeaway.)

'Go to sleep, Geri.'

'Yeah, sorry. G'night.'

'G'night. Hey, how about going to town tomorrow morning?'

'Sorry, can't. Hockey.'

'Oh yeah, I forgot. Afternoon then?'

'Yeah, we could ring Ellie and Shah first thing, arrange to meet them outside Top Shop at one. I'll go straight there after the match.'

'Cool. Night then.'

'Night.'

Geri was soon zizzzzing, but I lay awake until two.

This morning – weather freezing. Geri went off with games kit at nine o'clock. Neil said, 'Jolly hockey sticks!' Ha ha, NOT! Mum looking peaky.

To-do list — call Ellie
          call Shah
          call Dad to ask if Bud's OK

Started with Dad. Dad said Bud had practically dug his way down to Australia and now woofs with an Aussie accent. The Odor-eeze was nowhere to be found. He asked if I was having a good time.

'Here, Tiff, let me have another word with Ross,' Mum cut in, snatching the phone away.

'Listen,' she said to Dad, 'When I tell you I want more contact time, I'm not saying you're not making a good job of looking after Tiff, because you are. I just think that more time with me would do her good. She needs my advice on girly stuff . . .'

(Like the case of the vanishing boobs, for instance. But little does she know!)

'What d'you think, Ross? Don't you agree with me that a kid of Tiffany's age needs her mum?'

(Like strawberries need cream – not! Like a fish needs a bicycle. I read that somewhere.)

31

I called Shah on my mobile and asked her about this. 'Do I need to spend more time with Mum?'

'No way. You need to spend more time with your mates!'

I grinned to myself. Thanks, Shah! 'So do you and Ellie want to meet up with Geri and me for a mega spending spree?'

'Today?'

'Yeah, we've only got six more shopping days till Christmas.'

'Seven, including today.'

'Whatever. Meet at one outside Top Shop, OK!'

Shah said she would phone Ellie, but I said, no, let me.

'You sure about that?' Shah checked.

I was certain. Which shows how naïve I can be.

'Hi, Ellie.'

'Hey, Shah!'

'It's not Shah, it's Tiff.'

Long pause, then flat voice. 'Oh, hi.'

I was hoping she was over The Big Freeze of yesterday, but obviously not. 'We're all meeting up in town at one. D'you fancy coming?'

'Who's "we"?'

'Me, Geri and Shah.'

'Dunno. Maybe.'

'Oh, come on, Ellie. We can't go shopping without you! You're the expert!'

'I might be busy. I'll have to see.'

'Busy doing what?' I couldn't believe how snooty she was being.

'Gran's invited me to stay while Mum and Dad go to his firm's disco. I might go round early and wrap presents.'

'Listen, if you're getting at me because I didn't invite you to my sleepover, you can forget it. I had enough trouble persuading mum to have just one person, let alone three!' I was mad now, and didn't care who knew it.

'Who says I'm getting at you?' Ellie switched on her 'who, me?' voice. 'I'm only saying I might be doing something else when you three go shopping. Or I might not. Maybe I'll see you there.'

'Yeah, OK Ellie. Whatever.' Be like that then, I said to myself as I slammed down the phone.

Went back to *Marie-Nicole* for a bit, but wasn't in the mood.

Wonder how many real authors get writers' block. Wonder how much they earn, and what happens when their books get bought by Steven Spielberg and turned into films. Would like a book of mine to be a film with Brad Pitt and Jennifer Aniston. Jennifer could be Angelique, say, and Brad could be the count. I'd play Marie-Nicole as a child. Then we'd skip a generation and Jennifer would be playing Marie-Nicole as a woman.

We'd need a new male lead then, though. Maybe Matt Damon. There's no point wanting to be a writer if you don't think BIG! By the time I'm twenty-five I want to have made a million.

Mum's given me twenty quid to spend on presents. That's twenty plus ten I got from Dad and seventeen pounds fifty that I've saved up. 20 + 10 + 17.5 = £47.50p.

Present list :
  Dad — socks and Bart Simpson car ornament
  Mum — Body Shop exfoliator and shower gel
  Gran Jackson — cookery book
  Gran Little — cookery book
  Grandad — Elvis book
  Geri
  Ellie } hair accessories (home-made)
  Shah
  Scott — ?
  Neil — ?
Odds and ends —
  gold and silver pen
  glue
  glitter
  white card

It hasn't felt Christmassy before, but now suddenly it does! Seized by shopaholic fever! Fairy lights, fake snow, Father Christmas, here I come!

Saturday evening.
  The worst day of my life! Ever, ever!
  I can't believe it. Seven days before Christmas, and Geri and I fell out! It might seem a little thing, but my life has fallen apart. Can't write now.

Sunday, December 18th

Too upset to look up horoscope, which will only tell me to glam up and party with my mates.

Have been told off by Mum for moping, but she doesn't understand.

'For heaven's sake, Tiffany, get it together! What's one tiny, insignificant row? You know what they're like; they'll soon get over it and you'll all be best buddies again by school tomorrow!'

They might get over it, but I won't. That's the point.

Doesn't Mum realize that I'm sitting here by myself and the three of them are having a cool time next door? Yes, next door! At Ellie's Gran's house.

Dad was better when I spoke to him on the phone yesterday.

'Tell me what happened,' he said. 'But stop crying, cos I can't tell what you're saying.'

'I was meant to meet them at one (blub-blub). Outside Top Shop (blub), but they weren't there. They'd deliberately gone off without me!'

'What, all of them?'

'Yeah. Ellie (blub), Shah (blub) and Geri (blub).'

'Ah, babes, I'm sorry.'

Blub-blub-mega-blub.

Dad said to keep my chin up and he'd come and collect me at six on Sunday.

'Can't I come home now?' I wailed. I didn't want to be next door to the sleepover club.

'Best not,' Dad said. Meaning, that'd upset Mum.

So I was stuck in the flat, running end to end action replays inside my head.

I get into town at quarter to one, plenty of time. I walk to Top Shop. I wait.

It's one o'clock. No one shows up. It starts to rain. I pace up and down until one-fifteen. Maybe my watch is wrong. I check on the shopping centre clock. My watch is right.

OK, so Top Shop has more than one entrance. I go all around the block. Nope, just the one door. 'So This Is Christmas' blasts through it with a gush of warm air.

I feel sick.

Try them on the phone, I tell myself. I take it out and find the stupid battery is dead.

Now I'm nearly crying. They did this on purpose! I bet it was Ellie's idea. She's been a total bitch lately. Yeah, this is down to her!

I set off around tinsel town, reindeer and sleigh bells everywhere, everyone in Father Christmas hats.

'Hey, Tiff!'

I hear this voice I DO NOT want to hear.

It's Adam Pigg. 'You shoppin'?' he asks.

'No, I'm lyin' on a beach, what's it look like?'

'Can I come?'

'No.'

He walks with me anyway, past Woolworths and Boots. 'You lookin' for Ellie-Geri-and-Fuchsia?'

'No!'

'I seen them in Sock Shop.' Squealer informs me. He holds up a plastic bag with socks in. 'For my dad. They must sell a million pairs a day at Christmas.'

Like I could care less! I blank him out, but he still doesn't take the hint.

'It's the school disco on Wednesday,' he reminds me with a cock-eyed leer.

I go hot and then cold. Oh my God! Adam Pig is chatting me up! 'Don't even think about it!' I yelp.

I leave him stranded in the Arcade.

'What?' he squeaks. 'What did I say? Tiff, come back!' I don't. I'm running up the High Street, bumping into Father Christmases. It's two o'clock and I haven't bought a single present, not even a sheet of wrapping paper. I'm suffering from post-traumatic, friendship fallout shock.

Then I run into Scott and Nadia. SCOTT AND NADIA. That's how come all the showers and the deodorized trainers. I'm not the only one whose been practising kissy-lips in the mirror!

I don't like Nah-Nah Nadia and she makes it plain she doesn't like me by staring straight through me. Does she know I threw her note down the loo?

Scott tries to act cool, the idiot. He's got his hands in his jacket pockets and he's shivering with cold, but he won't let on. If he opens his mouth to speak, his teeth will rattle.

'Lend me your phone,' I tell him.

He walks on.

I follow. 'Go on, Scott. My battery's dead. I need yours!'

'T-t-tough!' (That's his teeth chattering). 'It's at home.'

That's it. I give up and trail back to the flat. No one's in except me.

An hour later, I hear noises in the street. I look out and see Geri, Ellie and Shah with loads of carrier bags, laughing and fooling around.

I breathe a sigh. It's all been some big mistake. They're coming to fetch me. But no, they turn into the drive next door to my mum's. Trust Geri, she's got the wrong house! What a shock they're gonna get when they ring the bell!

I scoot downstairs to warn them, just in time to see Ellie turning the key in the front door.

Geri turns and sees me gawping. 'Hey Tiff, what happened to you?'

'What d'you mean, what happened to me? I was there! Where were you?'

'We were there, at half-twelve, like we said.'

'We said one!' I gasped. Ellie was inside the hall and Shah was following.

A woman with dyed blonde hair was peering out, saying, 'Come in, come in and close the door. You're letting the heat out!'

'Yeah but we changed that,' Geri said.

'When? When did we change it?' I had steam coming out of my head.

'Ellie rang me at school after hockey. I said I could make it half an hour early, so she said she'd call you and Shah to rearrange it.'

'Well, she didn't!' I yelled. 'And I wonder why not!'

The posh blonde energy conserver had closed the door by this time, leaving me and Geri rowing on the drive.

'Oh come off it, Tiff, you're not saying Ellie left you out on purpose!'

'Yeah!' I shouted. My stomach felt as if it had tied itself in knots. 'It's to get her own back because I left her out of my sleepover!'

'Yeah, whatever!' Geri turned away.

'It's true. She never rang. I never got a message. That's Ellie for you!'

She faced me again. 'Tiff, you're paranoid, you know that?'

Big word, big insult. I stood in the rain with my mouth open.

41

'You are. You always think that people are getting at you when they're not – especially Ellie.'

'Yeah, take her side, why don't you?' I'd lost it, I admit.

Geri shook her head. 'You'd better calm down, then come in and say sorry.'

'No way! I'm the one who got left standing like a lemon outside Top Shop!'

'Yeah well, get over it, why don't you?' She waited a while, then shrugged. 'OK, Tiff, have it your way. I'm going into Ellie's gran's house now, whether you come or not.'

The door opened and shut. My stomach churned. I stomped off back here.

At five, Mrs Shelbourn rang Mum's bell. She asked for Geri's bag and explained that since there'd been a little quarrel, Geri would prefer to spend the night at her house with Ellie and Fuchsia. And wasn't it a coincidence that Mum had moved in next door. She was very pleased to meet her and welcome her to the neighbourhood.

What could Mum say? She handed over the bag and thanked Mrs S for helping to sort things out. 'I'll have a word with Tiffany,' she promised.

'Girls of this age are terrible for falling out, aren't they? It must be their hormones whizzing about.'

I was in my room, listening to every word. Me and my hormones didn't come out, not even to say goodnight.

This is the way I see it. We're in front of the Games Department notice board. Ellie overhears me fixing up my sleepover with Geri, and realizes that Mum has moved in next door to her gran. She arranges to stay on Manor Road and invites Shah along for the Saturday night, to show she doesn't care about my measly sleepover, cos she's got one of her own!

Then I play right into her hands by suggesting the shopping trip, which allows her to muscle in and mess up arrangements, leaving me out in the cold. It works like a dream. Better still, Geri and me have a big barney so they ALL end up at Ellie's gran's.

Geri told me not to take it personally, but how else can I take it? I feel kind of hollow.

I mean, I just lost all of my friends!

From ten o'clock this morning there was loud music coming from the attic window next door.

I bet they left the window open deliberately, so I could hear Shah laughing at Geri's jokes and Ellie rehearsing a dance routine for the band. 'Dig your right leg in. Point your left arm towards the ground. Look at your left hand . . .' That was Geri yelling instructions.

'Why don't you go and make it up?' Mum kept asking. It had finally hit her that I was hurting. Neil was out at the golf range, so she had time for me.

'Can't,' I sniffed.

'Why not?'

'Cos!' I couldn't even explain without blubbing again.

'Listen, Tiff.' Mum sat me down on the pale blue sofa. 'Has this got anything to do with me and – er – Neil?'

I shook my head.

'You're sure? I mean, I haven't had a chance to ask you and Scott how you feel about things. I'd hate to think that it was making you unhappy.'

I stared at Mum. She was looking great – cool streaks in her hair, mascara and lippy, bright eyes. 'Things' had taken ten years off her. So I attempted a smile and said, no, it was nothing to do with her and Neil. I was OK with that. It was just Geri and the others.

She gave me an extra ten pounds for presents and told me she had something planned for Boxing Day which was a secret, but it included Scott and me.

'Scott's got a girlfriend called Nadia,' I told her.

'Not Nadia Steele? I remember her from First School! Little dark haired girl who used to kick him under the desk when the teacher wasn't looking.'

'That sounds like Nadia,' I said, and we moved on.

Other low points:
* Ellie, Shah and Geri took Mrs S's pooch for a walk. They made sure I saw them by yelling and squealing when the Lurcher lurched through puddles and ran off with Shah.
* Neil was late for lunch. Mum was not amused. 'Your dinner would be in the dog if we had one!' They've already had one major row, after stupid Scott got lost on our school trip. Mum went hysterical and Neil didn't show enough sympathy. She booted him out, but he was back after a week.

* Decided Marie-Nicole was rubbish and tore it
  up. Massive writers' block. End of creative
  streak? Curtains for Tiffany Little, wannabe
  writer? 'Her imagination burned bright at the
  age of eleven, but her star faded when life events
  took their toll. She was a great talent wasted, a
  pre-teen casualty of the stresses and strains of
  the twenty-first century!'

Dad collected me at six. Free at last to hibernate
in own room with tube of Pringles and vid.

46

Monday, December 19th

Your stars – *Eek! Let go of that choccie and grab an apple instead. If you lay off that junk food, you'll feel fab at Christmas!*

Gym today. I huddled in a corner and got changed. No one noticed anything. Everyone talking about disco. Have decided not to go.

Tuesday, December 20th

Your stars – *Venus, planet of all things heart-shaped, enters your astrological house of love this week. If you've been lacking in the lurve department lately, this is about to change. Swoon!*

This can't go on! I'm sitting by myself, eating by myself and going home alone.

'What's up, Tiff?' Squealer asked. He saw me sneaking out of a side gate and followed.

'Get lost!' I told him.

Shah's been off school for two days, which means Ellie and Geri go around together

47

ignoring me – which Ellie is excellent at, as you'd expect. Like, she stops talking when I come into a room, then whispers something behind her hand. Or else, she dives to save a desk for Geri and forces me to sit at the front. Geri goes along with it.

'Cheer up, Tiff!' Dad said when I got home. 'It'll soon be Christmas!'

Which is the worst thing he could say.

'Dear Gabrielle,
Please help. I've lost my three best friends, and with the festive season coming up I'm really worried that I'll be left out of all the fun. What can I do? Tiffany, 11, Ashbrook'

'Dear Tiffany,
To lose one friend is unlucky, but to lose three is downright careless! I suggest you take a good look at yourself and ask what you did wrong. After all, you can't go thru life mislaying people like this! Contact Frenz Anonymous for more help.'

Mum rang.

'Tiffany, tell me the truth. Are you being bullied at school?'

'No Mum, it's nothing like that.'

'Only, you were so unlike your usual self at the weekend, it occurred to me that bullying could be part of the problem.'

'It's not. Anyway, I'm OK.'

'Don't be silly, you're not OK. Anyone can see that, even your dad! Sorry, that was a cheap shot. Now, when I say "bullying", I don't just mean being hit and pushed around. There's such a thing as an emotional bully too, you know. Is somebody getting at you and undermining your confidence?'

'No, honestly!'

'Because, I've been thinking, I should probably contact your group tutor to discuss the problem. What's her name? Is it Miss Thornhill?'

'Hornby. Mum, don't ring school, please!' My heart was thump-thumping at the idea of a one2one between them. 'No one's bullying me, OK!'

'Even so, Tiff, I still feel it might be a good idea to put your teachers in the picture over what's happened at home.'

'They already know,' I lied. 'Dad wrote and told them at the start of term!'

'Don't lie to me, Tiffany,' Mum said stiffly.

'Your father never picked up a pen to write so much as a birthday card!' There was a long pause, then she signed off. 'Leave it with me. If there's a problem at school, I want to get to the bottom of it.'

'Yeah,' I sighed. 'Bye.'

'Keep your chin up, Tiff.' She made a couple of kissing sounds then hung up.

Shah called.

'Can I come round?'

'When?'

'Now.'

'I thought you were ill.'

'Not that ill. Just a stomach bug. I'm over it.'

'Ellie and Geri haven't spoken to me since Saturday.'

'I know, I heard. Forget it. Can I come?'

'OK then. See you soon.'

Shah's a brilliant mate. She really is.

She didn't even mention Saturday. She brought a book she thought I'd like and a top I'd lent her.

'I'm bored!' she sighed, flinging herself full length on my bed, with her hands behind her head.

'Will you be back at school tomorrow?' I could've thrown my arms around her and hugged her. I would've done if I was French.

'Yeah, it's the disco. I'm not gonna miss that, am I? Y'know, I've watched six vids in two days!'

'Were they any good?' If she didn't want to talk about Saturday, then it was fine by me.

'No. Pants, every single one.'

('Dear Gabrielle,
One of my friends is back!'
'Dear Tiffany,
Lucky you! Be more careful with her this time around!')

'So, are you ready for Chrissy?'

'Nope.'

'Me neither.' I told Shah I hadn't handed out a single card, and we only had two more days of school left.

'It just so happens . . . !' She dived into her dalmatian rucksack (white fur, black spots) and pulled out some ~~fluorresant~~ – fluorescent (looked it up) lime green

51

card, some felt tips and loads of glitter in a tube. Soon we were making Chrimble cards like crazy.

'What are you wearing to the disco?' Shah wanted to know. (*snip, glue, sprinkle, blow*)

'Dunno. Might not go.' (*fold, crease, cut, colour*)

'Stop messing around. I wanna know, what're you gonna wear?' (*snip-snip*)

'I mean it. What's the point, if Geri and Ellie aren't speaking to me?' (*turn upside down, colour some more*)

'They'll get over it.' (*snip*)

'It's not them. It's me.' (*sniff*) 'Shah, d'you think I'm paranoid?'

(*Snip-snip-snippety-snip*) 'Don't ask me.' (Meaning, 'I don't want to get involved.')

('Dear Tiffany,
Remember what I said. You need to be careful with this friendship, so don't push your luck!')

'Yeah well, whatever.' I stepped back from the fifth card I'd made. 'How come yours are better than mine? This one looks as if someone's been sick on it!'

Shah laughed. 'So, Tiff, what're you gonna wear?'

Outfit for disco:
striped pink and silver top
denim mini skirt covered with badges
shoes — not sure yet
face gems
crystal nail varnish

Feel loads better.

Wednesday, December 21st

Your stars – Tis the season to be jolly, so make the most of your good mood. After all, this is your fave time of year!

Major tragedy – Nadia ditched Scott!

On the day of the school disco! She dumped him by the Year 11 lockers, in front of all his mates! I was there. I saw it.

She came right up to him and told him not to bother calling for her tonight, she was going with Sean Hewitt in Year 12.

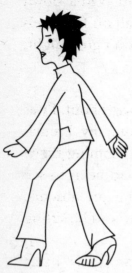

Just like that.

Scott blinked.

He didn't say anything as Nah-Nah-Nadia tottered off on her spike-heeled boots.

Well, what can you expect from a kid who used to kick you under the desk?

And all that deodorizing and taking showers for nothing!

Our family is taking a battering right now, what with me and my mates and Scott and his relationship blues.

'Ain't got no woman,
Ain't got no girl.
Ain't got no lover
In this whole wide world!'
Oh, Momma!

I left my brother blinking behind his locker door, trying to make out that his heart wasn't broken into a million tiny pieces. Nic Heron was with him, changing the subject and talking about last night's match on the telly.

I walked twenty metres behind Nadia down the corridor, praying for her to fall off her heels and sprain her ankle so she couldn't go tonight, and serve her right!

Anyway, I had my own stuff to worry about. I was heading for English in B14 from my French lesson in D6. Geri and Ellie were coming down from Design Technology. Shah had been to see Miss Hornby about not bringing an absence note. The big question was, who would be sitting where?

So I walked into the room with my heart pounding, looking like I couldn't care less. Ellie and Geri were already sitting in their normal back row seats, leaning across the aisle and comparing nail varnish. They saw me and blanked me out. So I stuck my head in the air and flounced past. My plan was to save a place near the front for Shah.

I sat down, put my bag on the next desk and waited.

'Hey, Tiff!' THAT voice grunted.

'Get lost, Adam!'

Squealer ignored me, turfed my bag off the desk and sat down next to me.

After Chucky Gilbert, Adam Pigg is the biggest pain in our year. He thinks he's funny and he's not. He's always getting on people's nerves – one of those small, skinny kids who looks about eight and acts like he's two and a half (i.e. having tantrums, punching, kicking, rugby-tackling). He's a Man U fan. Normally, if he sees a girl, he runs a mile.

But not today.

'Tiff, we can give you a lift tonight, if you want.'

I turn my head and stare out of the window.

'We drive by your house, so we might as well bring you.'

I flick my hair and give him a filthy look. 'That's Fuchsia's place!'

'Hornby sent her home to fetch a note, so I bagsied it. Anyhow, how about it?' Squealer has a lopsided face. His grin is crooked and he's got this habit of wrinkling his nose then pulling his top lip down over his teeth and up again – twitch, stretch, twitch. Not so much Pigg as rabbit.

'How about what?' I hiss. Mr Fox has just entered the room.

'The lift, stupid. D'you want one?'

I give him a withering look. 'Go boil your head!'

Gorgeous George overhears and gives me the Stare, the one he saves up for idiots stampeding down corridors. 'Tiffany!'

I'm beetroot red and trying to ignore the sniggers from behind. Adam Pigg just got me into trouble with my favourite teacher!

'Go boil your head!' Mr Fox echoes. 'That leads me nicely into our English Language topic for today which is the astonishing gift we all possess of choosing the right phrase to suit the occasion. Now, Tiffany could simply have said to Adam, "Go away", but that doesn't carry quite the same force as the charming expression which she did choose. In other words, she was angry. But in a way, she was also fairly restrained. After all, we can all think of stronger language, such as two words ending with "off"!'

A ripple of laughter went around the room. George always makes his lessons interesting!

'Now, Callum, I want you to give me the polite way of saying "Go boil your head". Imagine you're in a shop and the assistant comes up to you and puts you under pressure to make a purchase. What would you say?'

'Naff off!' Dom sniggers.

'Or, "No thank you very much, I'm not interested".' Mr Fox illustrates his point, sighs, then tells us to split into groups of four.

PARTY! PARTY! PARTY!

Shah came to my place to get ready.

I borrowed a pair of silver thong sandals from her. Dad said I'd catch my death.

Her hair looked fab. She sprinkled gold glitter in it and wore it up in a silver scrunchy. With a silver halterneck top and black, shiny combats. I gave her a silver badge with 'Teacher's Pet' printed on it. She pinned it on the seat of her trousers.

'How long are you two gonna be?' Dad shouted upstairs.

We'd been up there for two hours. I'd changed my hairstyle three times.

'What's the big rush?' I yelled down.

'Nothing. Only Nic just showed up. I'm taking Scott and him to the disco. Get a move on if you want a lift.'

Shah and I shot downstairs.

'Put your jacket on,' Dad said.

'Don't need it!' We glittered and glitzed in front of cool Nic.

Scott was still slouched in front of the telly, watching a Christmas Lottery special. Dad clicked the remote and stunned him into action.

'Hey, I didn't hear the Bonus Ball!' he moaned.

'Then we'll just have to put off being millionaires until next week.' Dad pulled him upright. 'Did you swipe my aftershave?' he asked suspiciously.

Scott grunted. 'Uh.'

'It smells like mine!'

'Uh.'

'Ask first next time, OK!'

'Uh.'

What was Mr Fox telling us about the astonishing gift we all possess?

In the van, I sat between Nic and Scott, with Shah up front with Dad.

'You girls look cool,' Nic said.

'D'you think he meant it?' I whispered to Shah, tugging at my denim micro skirt and flip-flopping through the main entrance. An icy blast of air brought me up in goose pimples.

'Swoon, swoon!' Shah replied. 'Isn't he funktastic?'

Everyone was in love with Nic. A gaggle of Year Elevens giggled up to him and we lost touch with our fave hunk.

In the drama hall, music was blasting out, lights were flashing, disks were playing, kids were dancing-pop-your-left-hip-out-and-tip-your-arms-and-head-to-the-left.

'Join the scrum!' Miss Westlake took our tickets at the door. 'Drinks are on the table near the stage.'

I'm all danced out.

Everything hurts – feet, eardrums, head . . .

Dad collected me at eleven and brought me home.

'Good time?' he asked.

I'd been trodden on, bumped, bashed and spilt over. 'Yeah, cool!' I sighed.

'Did you dance with any – B-O-Y-S?' The van rattled and shook my aching bones.

'Uh.' I'd hidden in the girls' loo from Squealer, Dom, Callum and Chucky Gilbert.

'Did you make friends with Geri?'

'Uh.' Yawn and groan. Geri had arrived with Ellie and the two of them had stuck together like glue.

Ellie's outfit – black sequinned top, silver trousers, hair up in twists and plaits. Hey, that was the style Geri and I had practised!

Geri's outfit – bright blue strappy top with silver star, blue combats, hair loose.

'You know what you should do?' Shah had suggested. 'I read this bit in a mag about texting a message to someone you've had a row with.'

We were in the loo at the time, hiding from Squealer. 'What message?' I checked my skin gems in the mirror and re-stuck a red one on my right cheek.

61

'You type in the text symbol for a rose, which is the 'a' with the circle thingummy round it, followed by two dashes, a more-than sign then two more dashes, like an arrow. Like this: @—>— Then you send it to your mate's moby number, imagining a bright pink light shooting from your moby to hers.'

'What's that supposed to do?'

'Heal the broken friendship, dimbo! Pink's the colour of love.'

'Yeah, like that's gonna work with Geri!'

Shah's a megatastic mate, but sometimes I think she has weird ideas.

'Did Scott enjoy himself?' Dad asked, as we turned the corner into our street.

'Uh.' Scott hadn't danced once. He was stuck in a corner with his mates, telling jokes and talking about footie. Nadia and Sean had smooched right in front of him.

Dad gave up asking questions, parked the car and followed me inside.

Thursday, December 22nd

Your stars – Leo lasses sometimes take their mates for granted. So why not make a special effort to make your best bud feel great today?

Last day of school!

Dived for the doormat before Bud could chomp the Chrissy cards. Opened them, read messages 'to Gina, Ross, Scott and Tiffany, with all our love, Jo, Keith and the twins' and 'to the Littles from the Dawsons, Happy Chrimbo!' etcetera.

Like we were all still one big happy family.

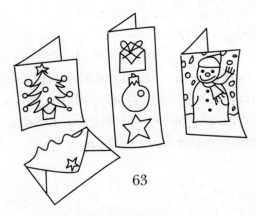

63

Fed Bad Breath and walked him in Clean It Up Zone. Luckily he didn't perform. I hate the plastic bag bit. Hmm, maybe Bud's breath stinks because he's constipated? What goes in must come out at one end or the other.

Got to school late, at same time as . . . MUM!!!!!!!!

Me:	(*gobsmacked*) Mum, what're you doin'?!!!'
Mum:	(*marching towards the office*) I've come to see Miss Hornbeam.
Me:	Hornby. (*running to bar her way*) What for? Stop! Don't do it!
Mum:	(*reaching past and ringing secretary's bell*) I'm worried about you, Tiff. I want to have a word with your teacher.
Secretary:	(*sliding back the glass panel*) Yes?
Mum:	(*in a posh voice*) I have an appointment with Miss Hornbeam – um – Hornby. I'm Gina Jackson, Tiffany Little's mother.
Me:	I told you not to! You're only makin' it worse!

Secretary:	(*pointing to a chair in the corridor*) Take a seat. I'll see if Miss Hornby's free. (*The glass panel slides shut. A bell rings. Pupils burst out of classrooms into the corridor*)
Miss Hornby:	(*striding down corridor in dark blue tracksuit, spies me hovering beside Mum*) Tiffany Little, why weren't you in registration?
Mum:	(*jumps to my defence*) I asked her to wait here with me. I'm her mother. I take it you're Tiffany's group tutor?

Phew, that got me out of a detention for being late. But it also roped me into being there when Mum had her one2one with Miss H.

We were in the Year Head's office, with timetables plastered all over the walls and books piled on the desk. Mum was wearing her grey work suit with a purple top and new high-heeled boots. Compared with the Tracksuit Queen, she looked cool. But I was squirming anyway.

'The thing is, Miss Hornby, Tiffany is going through a difficult time. Her father and I separated during the summer holidays.'

TQ nodded and made a quick note.

'We're still friends . . .'

They are? You could've fooled me.

'. . . But it's bound to be unsettling for Tiff and Scott.'

Unsettling, as in Scott slobs in front of the telly to mask the pain? As in, I get paranoid and lose all my buddies.

'Of course.' TQ nodded again. 'I'm glad you've informed us of the situation.' (Like, how come you've waited this long to tell us?)

'And just lately, I've been really worried about Tiffany. She seems to be having problems with friends, which she's never had before. She's always been a really popular girl.'

'What kind of problems?' Pencil poised, waiting to take more notes.

I was sinking lower in my plastic seat, trying to disappear.

'It's just that she seems a bit isolated. And you know what girls are like. They can be real little bitches at this age.'

That's my mum, breaking through the polite shell, telling it like it is!

Miss H flinched. She jotted something down. I stared at the timetables and gripped the sides of my chair. This was pure torture.

The bare lightbulb glared in my face. The woman behind the lamp wore a dark blue uniform. Her hair was scraped back in a bun, her eyes were hard and cold.

'Give me names!' she snapped, putting her face close to mine. Her skin gave off the smell of disinfectant.

'No way!' I gritted my teeth and held still tighter to my chair.

'Names!' she repeated. 'Or else!'

Or else what? Electric shock? Thumbscrews? The rack?

'Is there someone in particular who you think may be getting at Tiffany?' Miss H asked.

Mum turned to me. 'Tell her, Tiff.'

I shook my head. I'd rather rip out my own tongue.

'It's important. The school has to know what's going on if they're going to help.'

Another shake.

'Tiffany, if you don't tell Miss Hornby, I will!'

'No!' Like a rat in a trap, I bolted. Out of the door, down the corridor, up the stairs, through the library and out of the side door. It was snowing outside and just beginning to settle. Splashing through slush, I made it to the gate and out on to the main road, where I headed for home.

I skived off the last day of term, all because of Mum!

She followed me, natch.

'Oh Tiff, what's happening?' She was sitting on our lumpy sofa next to Bud. I was hunched up in the chair opposite.

We'd got through a box of tissues before either of us could talk. 'Is it my fault?' she sniffed.

I blew my nose. 'No.'

'Only, you have to accept that your dad and I have split up. We all have to move on.'

'I know.' Personally, I'd moved on from moping about Geri to feeling wrecked because my parents were at war. That was far enough, thank you!

'Leaving wasn't easy. It took me over a year to decide. But I knew you and Scott were old enough – it wasn't as if you needed me twenty-four hours a day any more.'

I blew again.

'And I knew I wasn't going very far.' Nod, sniff, dab, blow.

'And . . . I do miss you, Tiff . . .'

Blub, blub, blub! No more tissues, nothing more to say.

So, this is Christmas! Dad came home and took one look at me.

'Never mind, it's not the end of the world,' he said.

Friday, December 23rd
Christmas Eve Eve

Your stars – *Your mouth is already watering over the delish Chrissy treats on their way. So go ahead, chomp the cake, nosh the nuts and push in the pud!*

A big blub gets it out of your system. I feel fine now. There's three inches of snow outside. The world looks like a Christmas card. Bud went ballistic in the park.

<u>SNOWED UNDER</u>

Snowflakes feather my face
An icicle forms in my eye –
Little snow queen
Hardens her heart

White world freezes over
Feelings lie hidden from sight –
No melting moments
No distant light

Have broken through writers' block with this short poem about how I'm feeling deep down.

Maybe lines 2 and 4 in verse 1 should rhyme?

Mum's due to call here and take me guilt-trip shopping.

Text message from Shah. 'U OK? Skye hre for Chrimbo. Weird!'

Skye is the half-sister that Fuchsia has just found out about after eleven years of being an only child. That must do things to your personality. Shah's dad had a fling before he met Shah's mum. He never mentioned it until Skye got in touch and said she wanted to come for Christmas. The whole family was in shock at first. Then Shah's mum got over it and said Skye should visit. She's amazing like that, which makes Shah pretty cool too. They don't act mean like other people might. Wonder how Shah's dad feels?

Texted her back. 'I'm kool. Going 2 shops. See u in town?'

Shah to me – 'May-b. Depnds on S. See u!'

Mum and me went in on the bus. She came to the house and used her key, then bumped into Dad in the hallway.

'How's Tiff?' she whispered.

'Fine,' he said.

'And how are you?'

'Survivin'.'

Long silence. 'Christmas kind of brings it home, doesn't it?'

'Yeah, not easy.'

'Neil's spending Christmas Day morning with his ex and kids.'

Silence.

'What will you be doing?'

'Not a lot. Opening presents, taking the dog for a walk . . .'

'And Scott and Tiff can still come to me on Boxing Day?'

'That's what we said.' Dad's voice was fading as he went into the kitchen.

'Tiff!' Mum yelled upstairs. 'Let's set off before the snow gets worse!'

> *'Sleigh bells ring, are you listenin'?*
> *In the lane, snow is glistenin'.*
> *We sing a love song as we go along,*
> *Walkin' in a winter wonderland!'*

Mum and me shopped till we dropped. She

bought my main pressie, which is a silver padded jacket with a hood trimmed with white fake fur. I wore it round town for the rest of the morning. Scott's got new trainers. Plus small pressies like a CD, socks and boy bathtime stuff.

'He won't need that any more,' I told her. 'Nadia dumped him.'

Mum tutted. 'He still needs to smell nice, for next time.'

She stuffed sprays and lotions into her basket, including aftershave for Dad.

'What did Miss Hornby say when I ran off?' I asked, in the middle of the Body Shop checkout.

Mum raised her eyebrows. 'She panicked. I told her not to worry, I'd take responsibility for keeping you at home for the rest of the day.'

'You didn't mention Geri and Ellie?'

Mum shook her head. 'Honestly Tiff, you have this knack of making things worse for yourself.'

'Me?' I squeaked. 'What about you?'

'That's twenty-five pounds thirty.' The assistant held out her hand.

Mum handed over the dosh. 'I was only trying to help.'

'Well next time, don't!' I begged. 'This is between Geri, Ellie and me, OK!'

I think I got through to her at last. 'Miss Hornby doesn't seem like the sort who would listen anyway. Not exactly the sensitive type.'

'If you can't hit it with a racket, forget it,' I muttered, slipping and sliding on the icy street. Father Christmas went by on his sleigh. I waved at Ruth Miles, a girl in 7JT. I was looking out for Shah and Skye, but not having any luck.

'Honestly, this place is heaving!' Mum forged ahead through the crowd. 'People go mad at Christmas, buying everything in sight. I can't find a set of treelights for love nor money!'

We tried Woolies, Boots and Asda, but were still treelightless. 'Can we go home?' I moaned.

'What time is it? Oh no, we should've met Neil in the multi-storey car-park quarter of an hour ago!'

We blundered and skidded across town to find him champing at the bit.

'What time d'you call this?' He tapped his watch.

'Sorry!' Mum gasped. 'We forgot to keep a check!'

Neil zapped the central locking and opened the doors. Even on his days off he looked like he was at work – smart jacket, shiny shoes. 'Dump those in there and let's go,' he snapped.

I'm trying to like Neil. No, put that another way – I'm trying not to HATE Neil – but he doesn't make it easy, especially this next bit.

We were stuck in a traffic jam by the big building society offices. An electronic sign on the tower was telling us that it was –2 degrees centigrade, the radio weather forecast said more snow overnight. Neil was fuming at the wheel. Mum turned round to me in the back seat.

'Tiff, would you tell me exactly what this row with Geri and Ellie is about?' she said.

'You wouldn't want to know!'

'Yes, I would. I'm your mother!'

There was no escape. 'We were meant to meet up in town last Saturday at one o'clock, only Ellie rang Geri and Shah and changed it to half-twelve. She was supposed to ring me as well, but she never did!'

Neil's fingers drummed the steering wheel. He looked at his watch again.

'So I showed up at one and no one was there. It's Ellie's idea of a joke, but I wasn't laughing. Then Geri said I was reading too much into it and I yelled at her – all because of Ellie not ringing me!' It came tumbling out again, like it had only just happened.

'What're you on about?' Neil cut in. He was looking at me in his overhead mirror. I could just see his eyes and forehead. 'Ellie rang. I took the call.'

'What did she say?' I sat in the back gasping like a fish.

'She said she'd tried your mobile but it was out of service. She told me twelve-thirty instead of one o'clock. Didn't I pass on the message?'

'No, you didn't!' I wailed.

'Sorry, I thought I had.' Neil mirrored, signalled and manoeuvred from one lane to the next. The man behind beeped his horn.

So this was Neil's fault – every single nightmare moment! I'd lost two of my best mates in the whole world, all down to my mum's stupid boyfriend!

Friday afternoon – I went round to Shah's and met Skye. Weird, they don't look at all alike. That figures – Shah's mum is half Jamaican and Skye's mum is white. So is their dad. So Shah has this mega black, wavy hair, and Skye's is brown and straight. Skye's at sixth form college in Glasgow, studying psychology, English and sociology. Her voice is the most different thing about her. It kind of rolls around her mouth and goes up and down in different places to an English accent.

'Shah's told me a lot about you,' Skye said to me. 'She says you're the creative type. You make up stories.'

I nodded and mumbled. 'English is my best subject.'

'And poems and songs,' Shah insisted. 'She never talks about it, but she's really good. She wants to be a writer!'

Skye was sitting cross-legged on a cushion on the sitting-room floor. 'Cool!' she murmured.

I was feeling awkward, not really in the mood

for talking. My mind was still on stupid Neil. But I couldn't have a sesh with Shah while Skye was there.

Then the phone went. It was for Shah, which left me and Skye alone in a room smelling of essential oils and candles.

'Shah says you fell out with Geri and Ellie,' she said, looking at me with her head sideways.

She made me jump, bringing up the subject like that. But it came out really friendly and nice. So I nodded and looked miserable.

'Bummer,' Skye murmured. 'I hate it when that happens.'

I took a deep breath. 'Yeah, and I've just found out the whole thing is my fault!'

'No, really!' Skye sat there cross-legged, leaning against the radiator in her grey hoodie and black combats, with bare feet and her hair swinging in front of her face every time she moved her head.

So I told a complete stranger about my worst troubles.

'Huh!' she said. 'That sounds like it's down to Neil, so stop beating yourself up.'

'But I yelled at Geri and she said I was paranoid, which I looked up and basically it means you think the whole world is against you . . .'

'Yeah, we just did paranoia in psychology.'

'So am I paranoid then?'

'No way! Maybe a wee bit over-sensitive, but most of us are sometimes. So what're you gonna do next?'

I didn't have an answer.

Then Shah came back in, looking edgy. 'That was Geri,' she announced. 'She's invited me to a party at her place tomorrow night.'

My little world was about to fall apart all over again. There'd be no phone message for me, they would all be party-party-partying like mad without me!

'So this is how you handle it!' Skye said. 'You come round here and get ready with Shah. Dad takes you both round to Geri's place and drops you off.'

'But I'm not invited!' I reminded her.

'So what? You're there on the doorstep. You say sorry, it's all been a big mess. Geri says sorry too. There's a party going on inside, so you all go in and have a brilliant bash, Happy Christmas!'

Saturday, December 24th
Christmas Eve

Your stars – There's loads of planetary action in the friends part of your chart, which totally changes the way you interact with people. It's nice to let others help you out every now and then – even Leo gals need a break sometimes!

Skye made it sound so simple – I go to Geri's party and say sorry it's all been a big mess. And my star chart makes a thing of 'frenz' and all that. But I've got a million butterflies in my stomach and a whole day to get through before I do my 'sorry' bit. I keep thinking, What if . . .?

What if Geri slams the door in my face?

What if I get in but Geri and Ellie ignore me all night?

What if I ruin everyone's Christmas?

What if Dad opens his aftershave from Mum and breaks down and cries?

What if Mum rows with Neil and goes hysterical?

What if I can never ever EVER write anything EVER again?

In fact, why don't we cancel Christmas right now, before we go any further?

There was a heap of last minute cards on the mat. Bud got to them and chewed half of them up:

> *To Ross, —a, —ott and Ti—*
> *Love from*
> *Aunty Maureen and Unc– —ge*
>
> *xxx*

Scott counted and came up with a total of 136 cards altogether. Boys like to count, for some reason. Dad's customers send him cards – the little old ladies whose front porches he mends, and the man at the corner shop who needed a new wire shutter for his window. I personally got 38 cards from kids at school, not counting the one from Squealer which I threw straight in the bin. Callum saw me do it and said in a loud voice, 'Adam Pigg fancies you!' I withered him with a stone cold stare.

After breakfast this morning, Scott came up with his list for Santa Claus.

'Too late,' Dad said. 'The old man already set off from Greenland with his reindeer!'

'Yeah, yeah.' Scott put in his request anyway. 'I need a new computer.'

'Dream on,' Dad said, crunching his overdone toast.

'But I do, honest! I've got all these school projects and stuff to do on a PC – you get better grades at GCSE if you ponce them up with computer graphics and present them properly!'

Dad and I both knew he wanted to upgrade his PC so he could play more games, get a sound system included and spend the whole day on the Internet.

'Too late. I already bought your present,' Dad mumbled through the crumbs.

'Dad, hang on, listen!' Scott got ready to launch another attack. 'All the other kids have got . . .'

'All the other kids have got parents with money to burn. Watch my lips, Scott: I am not going to buy you a new computer, end of story!'

'Well, thanks a lot!' Since Nadia, Scott had slipped back into his grungy phase. He got up from the table with marmalade smeared down his front and his trousers at half-mast, as Gran

Jackson says. Meaning, just about slipping down over his bum, with the crotch around his knees.

'Never mind, Scott, Mum got you a pair of socks,' I sympathized. Socks was a kind of Christmas joke in our family. You'd sit and unwrap them with everyone looking and a note would fall out, saying, 'Oh no, not . . . socks!'

I say 'was' because it was Mum's idea. She bought us Simpson socks, South Park socks, Micky and Minnie Mouse socks, Superman socks . . .

Anyway, the joke wasn't funny when I said it at breakfast time. It just made us realize – well – things are different now.

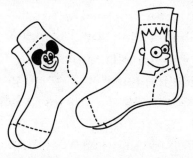

Spent the morning at the supermarket. Came back covered in bruises. Those old ladies who send Dad cards also elbow you out of the way at checkouts and stamp on your toes to get the last box of mince pies. Dad stands there and says, 'After you!' He also says, 'Look at the price of those crackers! What do they put inside – gold nuggets!' and, 'Tiff, any idea how you cook turkey?'

I came out feeling like a limp lettuce leaf, pushing a trolley full of stuff none of us knew how to cook, with three packs of ready-made lasagne, just in case our kitchen turned into a disaster area.

'At least we won't starve,' Dad said. He always looks on the bright side.

At home again, unpacking the shopping while Scott scoffed all the Kettle Chips that were meant for tomorrow teatime, Shah called me on my moby. 'Hey Tiff, did I tell you the party is fancy dress?'

Eek! I'll be standing on the doorstep saying sorry dressed as Burglar Bill or a traffic light! 'No,' I squeaked. 'Listen Shah, maybe I won't . . .'

'Don't be stupid, course you're coming!

I've got stuff here at my house. Skye's gonna help us get ready.'

'Yeah but I'm really nervous. What if . . . ?'

The phone went dead before I could start on my nightmare list.

'What's up, Tiff? Has the world come to an end?' Dad tossed a bag of frozen peas at me, then rugby-tackled Scott to rescue the Kettle Chips.

'Yes,' I told him, whacking the peas into Scott's hands. I poised ready to flounce upstairs. 'As a matter of fact, since you bother to ask, it definitely has!'

'Come round to the flat and have a look.' Mum had listened to me and come up with a suggestion.

I'd asked her if she'd got any eighties gear at the back of her wardrobe that I could wear for my fancy dress. I was that desperate. 'Y'know, glam rock stuff, big shoulder pads, curly wigs.'

She'd laughed. 'You're talking a bit before my time!'

'No! You were 15 in 1980, you're always talking about Abba.'

'Yeah, OK, don't rub it in. Only, I don't know what I chucked out when I moved here. Maybe I got rid of it all.'

So in the end she said it was best to see for myself.

I walked to Manor Road and Nightmare Neil answered the door. For once he was dressed in scruffy jeans and a T-shirt, like a normal person. 'Come in if you can get in,' he said. 'We've had a crisis – a burst water pipe. Gina's panicking in case we can't get our water supply back before Christmas, so I'm on my hands and knees under the kitchen sink, trying to mend it.'

'Mum?' I yelled, making it clear I didn't care about Neil's smelly pipes. Not after what he'd done to me!

'In the loo!' she yelled back.

'Sorry about yesterday,' Neil said, out of the blue. 'I was a right grumpy sod, wasn't I?'

I couldn't believe my ears. Had he just said the 'sorry' word?

'Your mum says that me not passing on that message caused a lot of bother between you and your mates?'

I sniffed then nodded.

'Yeah well, I'm sorry about that too. It's just that I had a lot on my plate. I didn't mean to upset anyone.'

'It's OK,' I mumbled. I managed it with my teeth firmly clenched, so it came out like I didn't mean it.

'You and I haven't exactly hit it off, have we, Tiff?' Neil went on. 'Course, I understand it's hard for you to get used to having me around ...'

Oh no! Neil was turning into a nice guy! I couldn't cope. Then Mum came out of the bathroom and rescued me. 'I dug some stuff out from the packing cases still in the spare room. Come and look.'

She whisked me off and showed me bright purple flares and silver wedgies, a short little shiny black top with tapering sleeves, a pink feather boa and massive gypsy earrings.

'Cool!' I whispered when I saw them all laid out on the bed. That's great, Mum. Thanks!'

I learned a lesson from Neil of all people. Namely, that saying a big SORRY doesn't make you go up in flames or change you into a slimy frog. In fact, it turns you from Mr Nasty into Mr Nice, just like that!

'Sorry!' I rehearsed in front of the mirror at Shah's house, dressed up in my glam rock gear. My bright red mouth made a round 'O', then stretched wide and flat for the 'Y'.

'See, that didnae hurt one bit!' Skye laughed. 'S-O-double R-Y!'

'Sorry-sorry-sorry!' I gabbled. 'Geri, Ellie, it was all my fault. I messed up. I was stupid. Will you be best mates again?'

'Never grovel,' Skye advised. 'It doesn't look good. People won't respect you.'

I tried again, more casually. 'Sorry about last Saturday. Only, I never got the message, thanks to Neil.'

'Don't blame anyone else,' was Skye's comment. 'It makes you sound bitter and twisted.'

It was like she was giving marks out of ten for Apologizing – the new Olympic event.

'OK.' I stared straight into the mirror and took a deep breath. 'I'm sorry. How's that?'

'Brand new!' Skye laughed. Which is Scottish for 'perfect, ten out of ten'!

I was still shaking like a leaf outside Geri's house, though.

Those 'what ifs' were making me wobbly.

'Ready, pardner?' the American cowgirl standing next to me asked. Shah's dad had hitch-hiked round the world when he was a student and brought back a real stetson and red and white cowboy boots from Arizona. Her mum had given her a denim shirt and jeans, then Skye had made a giant belt buckle out of cardboard and silver foil. The kid next door had lent her a plastic holster and a toy gun.

'Ready!' I nodded.

Shah rang the bell.

I looked up at the holly wreath on the

door. 'Sorry! Sorry!' I kept on saying under my breath. This was worse than the dentist's, washing up and SATs tests combined!!!

The holly wreath shook and the door opened.

Geri and Ellie stood there without a stitch of fancy dress on them. They stared at the cowgirl and the eighties chick.

I filled my lungs with air. 'I'm . . .'

'. . . Dressed up!' Geri exclaimed.

'No. Sorry. I'm sorry!' I gasped.

'But you are dressed up, aren't you?' Ellie stepped outside and looked us up and down to make sure.

'Of course we are. That's what Geri said we had to do!' Shah frowned at Ellie and Geri's normal party wear.

'Yeah, but I rang later to say we'd changed our minds and not to bother with the fancy dress!' Geri grabbed Shah's hat and tried it on.

'Who did you tell?' Shah demanded.

'Your dad. Didn't he pass it on?'

I looked at Shah and she looked at me. 'No!' she said.

'That's men for you.' Ellie was starting to smile.

'Right!' I'd got over my nerves now. 'That's exactly what happened to me last Saturday. The message never got through!'

'Hey!' Geri kept the hat on. 'Say that again, Tiff!'

'I NEVER GOT THE MESSAGE ABOUT HALF-PAST TWELVE!' I said in capital letters.

'Y'mean, we fell out over nothing?' The light dawned on Geri.

I nodded. 'I'm still sorry I acted like I did.'

'Me too. Like, really sorry. This week has been lousy.'

I nodded and breathed deep.

'Hey, let's all make up and forget about it!' Ellie was dragging Shah and me into the house.

'But we can't come in dressed like this!' I squeaked, wobbling over on my wedgies.

'Yeah, you can, it's funky!' Geri insisted. 'Specially you, Tiff.'

'They're my mum's,' I admitted, twiddling my boa.

'And these are my dad's.' Shah stuck one boot under Geri's nose. Geri grabbed her leg and pulled her inside.

So Shah hopped and I wobbled into the party.

Everyone was there. We had music, singing and disco dancing. We had karaoke and games, food, food and more FOOD. Balloons got burst, crackers got pulled, we wore paper hats and told bad jokes. 'Question: What do you call an eskimo's house without a toilet? Answer: An ig.'

Then we went home.

Sunday, December 25th.
Christmas Day

No stars.

Happy Christmas Dad, Happy Christmas Scott, Happy Christmas Bad Breath, Happy Christmas everyone!

h *Another title by Jenny Oldfield*
from Hodder Children's Books . . .

Definitely Daisy 1
You're a disgrace, Daisy!

Meet Daisy Morelli – a magnet
for trouble and a master plotter.
When things go wrong – and they
always do – who gets the blame?
Definitely Daisy!

Daisy's fed up with school, so
she plans to run away – chucking
in boring lessons for footballing
stardom! If only the junior
Soccer Academy will have her . . .